GAIJIN

AMERICAN PRISONER OF WAR

a graphic novel by Matt Faulkner

Disney • HYPERION
LOS ANGELES NEW YORK

First Edition, April 2014
10 9 8 7 6 5 4
FAC-029191-18222
Printed in Malaysia

Library of Congress Cataloging-in-Publication Data
Faulkner, Matt.
 Gaijin: American prisoner of war / Matt Faulkner. —First edition.
    pages cm
 Summary: After the attack on Pearl Harbor in 1941, a thirteen-year-old California boy who is
half Japanese is sent to an internment camp. Story based on the history of the author's great-aunt.
 Includes bibliographical references.
 ISBN-13: 978-1-4231-3735-1
 ISBN-10: 1-4231-3735-3
 1. Japanese Americans—Evacuation and relocation, 1942–1945—Juvenile fiction. 2. Graphic
novels. [1. Graphic novels. 2. Japanese Americans—Evacuation and relocation, 1942–1945—
Fiction. 3. Racially mixed people—Fiction. 4. World War, 1939–1945—United States—Fiction.]
I. Title.
 PZ7.7.F39Gai 2014
  741.5'973—dc23   2013029795

Reinforced binding
Visit www.DisneyBooks.com

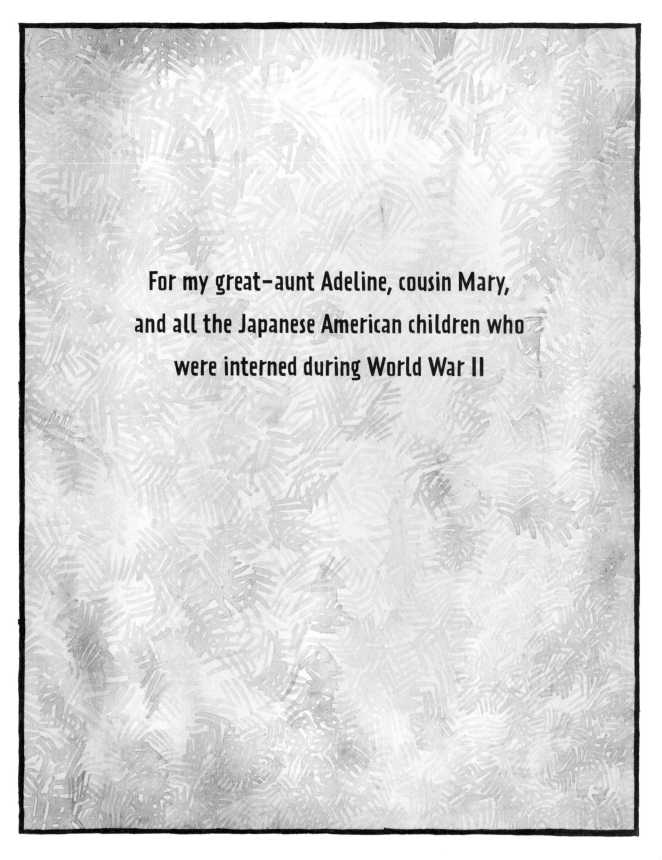

For my great-aunt Adeline, cousin Mary,
and all the Japanese American children who
were interned during World War II

Maybe Pop *was* flyin' one of those planes.

Just before dawn...

What the...?!

See you later, alligator!

Pop! Wait! Come back!

In the cafeteria...

Hey, Jappo.

...and after school.

Wait up!

All aboard.

Hold on there, sport. The car is full.

It's not full. There's plenty of room in there!

Not for you, there isn't!

No Japs in my car.

Hey, that ain't fair!

Oh, ya? Well, take it up with Emperor Hirohito!

Sayonara, slanty eyes.

Much later...

Next.

Finally.

You see, Koji was born in San Francisco! He's as American as you and me! The letter must've been a mistake, right?

Mistake? There was no mistake.

As I'm sure you know, Mrs. Miyamoto, the United States is at war with Japan. Your son, Koji, is half Japanese. Therefore, he will be placed in an assembly center. It's for his own good, really.

For his own good?! Are you nuts? He's only 13 years old.

Listen, buster, you are not going to send my son to a prison camp all by himself! Got it?

After breakfast...

Sorry, but I don't have a single blanket left. I gave the last one to the infirmary yesterday.

Thanks anyway.

I'm going over to the infirmary to see if they need help. Wanna come?

Nah. Think I'll just take a walk.

Hey, little guy. Whatcha up to?

Playin' marbles.

COMMANDER'S QUARTERS

The following morning...

Let's go straight to breakfast, OK?

Don't you want to use the men's latrine first?

Nah, the place gave me the creeps.

Mornin', chief.

What ya got?

Spam and powdered eggs!

This stuff isn't half bad.

You can have mine.

Good morning. How about we go fix that window?

Sure.

The next day...

Rabbits can be very destructive. This fence will keep them away from our vegetables.

But what about those?

Rabbits have to eat too, don't they?

I get it. The rabbits go after those and leave ours alone. Swell.

C'mon, Ma, let's go eat!

Koji! You're in the paper!

The camp newsletter has a story about you and Mr. Asai and the Victory Garden you've planted!

Good job, son. Put 'er there.

I'm not your son.

Koji!

I'll see ya later, Ma.

What'd I say?

Early the next morning...

Please be careful, Yoshi.

I will, Hana. Don't worry.

MEN

Good morning. I'm sorry to wake you.

G'mornin'.

It's no bother, Yoshi. How can we help you?

I've been given two passes to visit my home in the city. I wondered if Koji would like to come with me.

The next morning...

Hello, Mrs. Asai.

G'morning, Koji.

Mr. Asai is not feeling well today.

Will he be OK?

Oh, yes.

We were gonna work on the garden.

Why don't you go over to the grandstand and look at the new school?

ALAMEDA DOWNS

After lunch...

Not again!

Hey, gaijin! I hear your mama's hot to trot!

Ya! She's a real floozy!

Take that back!

Who's gonna make me?

Ooooof!

I said take it back!

Hey!

You boys! Break it up!

The dinner bell rang...

H'lo, Ma.

Koji!

Why're you cryin'?

Did you make her cry?

Me?

Keep your hands off my ma!

Koji! What are you talking about?!

Come back!

There's a kid on the fence!

Get him down and bring him to the commander.

Let's go, wise guy.

That evening...

Your son tried to climb over the fence this afternoon.

The commander wants to see you both tomorrow at 9 a.m.

Koji?

What!
Oh, man, you
scared me.

Could you help me
with packing up the garden
tools?

Sorry. Can't. Gotta go.

I'll give you something to cry about!

Let go of me, Mas!

The following morning...

Thank you for everything, Mr. and Mrs. Asai.

You're welcome, Koji.

Ma.

That afternoon...

Greetings!

Tomorrow we move to Camp Agua Dulce! Let's give a rousing cheer, shall we?

Hip hip...

Hooray!

Cough.

Yes... well.

That is all.

Mr. Asai, can I ask you a question?

Certainly.

The next morning, dozens of trucks and buses carried 8,000 Japanese Americans to Camp Agua Dulce.

San Francisco, 1946.

Tokyo, 1947.

The End.

Acknowledgments

The author would like to say thank you to:

My wife, Kris. Your love, support, and humor made this book possible. Thank you so.

My agent, Jennifer Laughran.

My editor, Rotem Moscovich, and designer, Tanya Ross-Hughes.

All the many friends, too many to name here, who shared articles, books, personal history, and support for this project.

My mother, Ruth, for keeping Adeline's story alive all these years.

My cousin Anita and all the "Adeline Cousins." Obachan Adeline would be so happy that we found each other!

Finding Adeline

Adeline Conlan, my great-aunt, was a celebrated Irish American singer in 1920. Against her parents' wishes, a teenaged Adeline joined a renowned vaudeville troupe and traveled the world. On a tour of Japan, she fell in love with and married Ichiro. Not long after, they had a baby girl named Mary.

During the late 1920s and early 1930s, attitudes toward Westerners and gaijin (outsiders) made life difficult for Adeline and Mary; tensions rose between Adeline and Ichiro. When an enormous earthquake shook Tokyo in 1923, killing thousands, a terrified Adeline decided that she and Mary would travel back to Boston, her hometown. They planned to return to Japan when things calmed down.

Unfortunately, they made the long journey from Japan to Boston only to find they weren't accepted there, either. Mary was ridiculed for being "half-caste." Adeline was ostracized for marrying outside her race and religion. Once again, they packed their things and moved, this time across the country to California, where they made a home in the Los Angeles area.

When she grew up, Mary became a wife and mother of two children. After the attack on Pearl Harbor by the Japanese navy, Mary and her babies received a letter from the United States War Office informing them that, because they were part Japanese and lived in the exclusion zone on the West Coast, they would be "interned" for an undetermined length of time. Irish American Adeline was not required to go to the internment camp, but she was not about to let her child and grandchildren be taken away from her.

On the first day of June 1942, Adeline and her family joined over 10,000 Japanese Americans from California and Washington and traveled the hot, dusty road to Owens Valley, California, where they were interned in the Manzanar War Relocation Center. Over two thirds of those interned at Manzanar were American citizens by birth. More than half of the 120,000 who were interned in the ten main camps during the war were children.

Adeline and her family lived in the camp for over a year. In the autumn of 1943, they found a sponsor and were allowed to move to Chicago. During the war, internees were encouraged to move eastward, away from the exclusion zone, if they had a good record and an established sponsor to speak for them. After the war's end, they were allowed to move back to California. Neither

Adeline nor Mary ever went back to Japan. And, sadly, although she and Ichiro exchanged letters, Adeline never saw her husband again.

In the late 1990s, I began to consider making a graphic novel based on the history of my great-aunt. All I had to go on was the return address on a corner of an old envelope shown to me by my mom when I was a kid. I did some searching on the internet; but for many years, I couldn't find Adeline or her family.

The Friday on which I turned in my first set of sketches to my editor, I found a post on the National Park Service–Manzanar website asking for anyone who might be related to Adeline Conlan to contact Anita, her great-granddaughter. I literally jumped when I read this.

I e-mailed Anita right away. Not long after, my son, Gabriel, and I drove to southern California to see a side of our family with whom we'd lost contact nearly forty years before. On the way there, we stopped for a day at the remains of the Manzanar War Relocation Center, now a National Historic Site. It was hot, maybe 100 degrees. As we stood in the shade of a withered tree, the wind howled and whipped dust into our eyes, and I marveled at the fortitude of those who had been interned there, prisoners in their own country.

Matt Faulkner
Southeastern Michigan
2014

Adeline Conlan and her family, Japan, mid-1920s

Selected Resources

BOOKS AND PERIODICALS

Fugita, Stephen S., and Marilyn Fernandez. *Altered Lives, Enduring Community: Japanese Americans Remember Their World War II Incarceration.* Seattle: University of Washington Press, 2004.

Ishizuka, Karen L. *Lost & Found: Reclaiming the Japanese American Incarceration.* Champaign: University of Illinois Press, 2006.

Japantown Task Force. *San Francisco's Japantown.* Mount Pleasant, S.C.: Arcadia Publishing, 2005.

Manbo, Bill, photographer. *Colors of Confinement: Rare Kodachrome Photographs of Japanese American Incarceration in World War II.* Edited by Eric L. Muller. Chapel Hill: University of North Carolina Press, 2012.

Price, Willard. "Unknown Japan," *National Geographic Magazine,* August 1942.

Styling, Mark. *Corsair Aces of World War 2.* Oxford: Osprey Publishing, 1995.

Time/Life Publications. *Our Finest Hour: The Triumphant Spirit of America's World War II Generation.* New York: Time/Life Publications, 2000.

DOCUMENTARY FILMS

Burns, Ken, producer. *The War.* PBS Broadcasting: New York, 2007.

Satsuki, Ina, PhD, producer/project director. *Children of the Camps— The Documentary.* PBS Broadcasting: New York, 1999.

WEB SITES

Manzanar National Historic Site:
   http://www.nps.gov/manz/historyculture/japanese-americans-at-manzanar.htm

Manzanar, Virtual Museum Exhibit:
   http://www.nps.gov/history/museum/exhibits/manz/imgGal.html

Children of the Camps, Internment History:
   http://www.pbs.org/childofcamp/history/index.html

Smithsonian Education, Letters from the Japanese American Internment:
   http://www.smithsonianeducation.org/educators/lesson_plans/japanese_internment/index.html